PUFFIN BOOKS

HAUNTING FOR BEGINNERS

Jenny Alexander lives in North Cornwall with her husband and four children. She took up writing when her youngest child started school. *Haunting for Beginners* was previously published as *Miss Fischer's Jewels*.

SURFERS

Haunting for Beginners

Jenny Alexander

Illustrated by
Michael Reid

PUFFIN BOOKS

PUFFIN BOOKS

Published by the Penguin Group
Penguin Books Ltd, 27 Wrights Lane, London W8 5TZ, England
Penguin Putnam Inc., 375 Hudson Street, New York, New York 10014, USA
Penguin Books Australia Ltd, Ringwood, Victoria, Australia
Penguin Books Canada Ltd, 10 Alcorn Avenue, Toronto, Ontario, Canada M4V 3B2
Penguin Books (NZ) Ltd, 182–190 Wairau Road, Auckland 10, New Zealand

Penguin Books Ltd, Registered Offices: Harmondsworth, Middlesex, England

First published as *Miss Fischer's Jewels* by Hamish Hamilton Ltd 1996
Published in Puffin Books 1998
1 3 5 7 9 10 8 6 4 2

Text copyright © Jenny Alexander, 1996
Illustrations copyright © Michael Reid, 1996
All rights reserved

The moral right of the author and illustrator has been asserted

Filmset in Bembo

Made and printed in England by Clays Ltd, St Ives plc

British Library Cataloguing in Publication Data
A CIP catalogue record for this book is available from the British Library

ISBN 0-140-37580-5

Contents

Chapter One
The Terrible Day

HANNAH STONE WAS not a girl who liked to show her feelings. If she was angry or upset, she would never throw a tantrum or burst into tears. She left all that sort of thing for her big sister, Beth. One person in the house going off the deep end all

1

the time was more than enough, her parents said – and Hannah agreed. If she had a problem, she would take herself off into a quiet corner, and wait grimly for the bad feelings to pass.

So on the day she had to part with Sherbert, she said not a word, even though her heart was breaking. She groomed him, and saddled him up. She took him out, for the last time, through the woods and up on to Cheriston Moor.

He had been Beth's horse really, given to her by a school friend whose family couldn't keep him any more, because they were moving to the city. Mum and Dad hadn't wanted to let Beth accept him, because they were worried about the cost of keeping him. But Beth had ranted and raged as usual, until she got her own way.

Dad said it wouldn't be long before Beth lost interest in him anyway; they could manage for a couple of months, and then sell him. But it was more like a couple of weeks before Beth decided that having a horse was too much like hard work, so Hannah stepped in to look after him, until they could find a buyer. And Hannah fell in love with him.

For five wonderful weeks, Sherbert had been Hannah's horse. But now a buyer had been found, and Sherbert was going to a different stables. Hannah's parents were relieved, for money was tighter than ever since the new supermarket had opened, and Dad's mobile shop was losing business. And then, to top it all, there was the roof . . .

Hannah came sadly back into the stable yard, and took Sherbert into his stall. She took off his saddle, and rubbed him down. She fed him and then, with a small sigh, she kissed him on the neck and turned away. She stood in the yard drinking hot chocolate with the other girls, until her mother came to collect her.

"Of course," her mother said, as they drove out into the lane, "you can still always come up here for a ride if you feel like it. Mrs Deacon's bound to be able to find you a horse."

Hannah gazed out the window at the fields flashing by, and thought, "I'll never go back there again. How could I?" For if she did, she would always remember Sherbert, and that would be too hard for her to bear.

As they came into the outskirts of Cheriston, Hannah's mother gave up trying to make her feel better, and they finished the journey in silence. Hannah was glad. It was bad enough that they had sold the horse – it would be even worse if they expected her to be cheerful about it.

They turned into Chestnut Grove. Hannah's house was a little bungalow, set well back from the road in its own large garden. It was quite old and tatty, but Hannah had always thought that it was perfectly fine. She looked at it now with a different eye. She saw that house as the cause of her unhappiness. For if it hadn't been needing a new roof, perhaps the family could have afforded to keep Sherbert. As it was, they were already going without crisps at playtime, cakes at tea-time and pocket money, in order to pay off the loan, and there was not a penny left to spare.

For a long time, Hannah stayed in the car. Her mother went indoors to make the tea. She knew that Hannah needed to be alone. For years, she had just been grateful that Hannah never made a fuss like Beth. But now she was beginning to worry about her, in case she was becoming too passive and withdrawn.

Outside in the car, Hannah stared at the house. The bad feelings churned around inside her like dirty clothes in the washing-machine. She didn't want to get them out. If she did, she might say rude and hateful things, and make it worse. She sat there, absolutely still, and nobody who didn't know her well could possibly have guessed how upset she was.

Eventually, she followed her mother into the house. On the floor in the corner of the living room, there was a mixing bowl, underneath the place where the first drips had started coming through the ceiling. It had been there for a while, and was covered with dust. She remembered how, at first, it had seemed like fun, waiting for the rain to come, listening to the drips. Now, she hated that stupid bowl. She would like to smash it in the fireplace. With a sigh, she went through into her bedroom.

Hannah shared a room with Beth. She had never minded that. When they were younger, they had played together all the time. Then, the room had been full of Sindy dolls and Lego houses. Now, Beth was nearly fourteen, and she didn't want to play any more. The Sindys were in a box under Hannah's bed. Beth's bed was like a ship adrift on an ocean of strewn tights and knickers, school books, boxes of talcum powder and used tissues. Eye pencils and pots of blusher were scattered across her bedside table, with bits of cot-ton-wool, stained pink, or brown, or blue.

All these things that came with Beth's

growing-up, Hannah had found rather glamorous. But she looked at them now with a different eye. They were spoiled, as her whole life was spoiled, by the loss of Sherbert. Now, instead of seeing lots of exciting things that she would grow into one day, Hannah looked at her sister's side of the room, and saw only a horrible mess.

"Hi!" Beth said. She was sitting on her bed, painting her toenails with bright pink nail varnish. "What's up?"

She had forgotten that today was The Day. The Terrible Day. How could she? It just showed how much Beth cared about Sherbert, Hannah thought, bitterly. It just showed how much she cared about anyone!

9

Hannah walked out of the room. Her feet were heavy, like her heart. She went through the kitchen, and opened the back door. Slobber, the dog, looked up at her, but even he knew when she was in a leave-me-alone mood. She crossed the uneven patio, and strode across the lawn.

The grass was ankle-deep, with daisies and dandelions growing in vigorous clumps all over it. There were trees. The flower-beds had nettles and brambles springing up amongst the bedding plants. It wasn't that no one in the family liked gardening. It was that they all liked the garden to be a little wild. Mr Stone said that Nature was the best gardener you could have. But whereas before it had been like a magical jungle, now, to

Hannah, the garden, like everything else, was only a horrible mess.

In the farthest corner of the garden, there was an old potting-shed. Hannah pushed open the door. Grass and moss grew abundantly on all the shelves. There was a damp and earthy smell. It was a soothing smell. This was the place Hannah always came, when things got bad, like when Beth went berserk over something, and Mum and Dad had a row about how to deal with her. Hannah sat down on the broken concrete floor, and stared into space.

Probably, she would have stayed there until bed-time. But pretty soon she heard a familiar noise from the other side of the wall. Snip. Snip. Miss Fischer was pruning her roses.

"Hannah," she said, softly. "Are you there?"

How did she know?

"Yes," Hannah replied.

"Was it terrible, darlink?"

She hadn't forgotten! Miss Fischer, who forgot everything, had remembered what was happening to Hannah on this day. Hannah was touched. She came out of the potting-shed and climbed on to the wall.

"No, it wasn't too bad," she said.

She dropped down into Miss Fischer's garden, light as a cat. Her face gave nothing away, but inside, she was kicking and screaming and bursting apart, with anger and grief and dismay.

Chapter Two
A Friend in Need

Miss fischer was wearing a green silk
dress that reached almost to the ground.
She was old, and rather fat, and her feet,
in their tiny black shoes, looked too small
to hold her up. Her hair was quite white,
except for one broad stripe of black,

which swept up across it like the plumage of some exotic bird. She wore lots of pale face powder, and bright red lipstick. Around her neck hung a long string of pearls.

"Did you ride him, darlink, one last time?" she asked.

To hear her speak, you would almost think Miss Fischer was English. She worked very hard at sounding English. The only thing that really gave her away was that hint of a 'k' at the end of 'darling'. However much she tried, she simply couldn't get rid of it.

"I did ride him," Hannah managed to say.

Hannah had known Miss Fischer since she was six years old, when she and Beth used to dare each other to climb over the wall. They were both terrified of her then, of course, with her strange, exotic clothes, and her loud, booming voice. But the first time she caught them in her garden, she wasn't angry with them. She gave them cherries and lemonade, and told them stories about her young days. Perhaps she was lonely, living all on her own. She invited them to call on her again, any time they liked. Beth soon lost interest in her, but Hannah loved going, and they grew very fond of each other. It was a bit like the way things turned out with Sherbert, when you came to think about it. When Beth got bored with the horse, it was Hannah who came to look after him and love him.

"It's nice of you to remember," Hannah said. "Beth didn't."

She couldn't keep the bitterness out of her voice.

"Perhaps she has other things on her mind," Miss Fischer suggested.

"Like painting her toenails?" said Hannah, coldly.

"I expect your poor parents . . ."

"You know what I think?" Hannah interrupted her. "I think my parents should never have agreed to take on a horse, if they couldn't afford to keep it."

Miss Fischer raised her eyebrows.

"If I remember rightly," she said, "they only let Beth have the horse because they didn't expect to have to keep him for long. They weren't to know that you

16

would fall in love with him! And they certainly didn't know that the roof would suddenly need replacing, did they?"

"Well, they should've done," Hannah said, unreasonably.

Miss Fischer sighed.

"I want to tell you something," she said. "Come inside, and we'll have a cool drink."

"You'd better tell me here, if it's important," Hannah suggested. "If we go inside, you'll forget to tell me at all."

Miss Fischer laughed. It was so true! She was incredibly forgetful. How often she had gone all the way to the shops, only to find she had forgotten her purse! Or made a splendid tea, only to remember that she had forgotten to invite anyone. This forgetfulness was one of the reasons why she was so fat – she would often forget she had had her dinner, and have another one! It wasn't that she was silly or vague. The problem was her enormous vitality. She was always so keen to move on to the next thing, that she often forgot to finish the thing she was doing.

She sat down on the garden seat, and patted the space beside her with her hand. Hannah came and sat down, too. She was comfortable with Miss Fischer.

"Many years ago . . ." Miss Fischer began.

Hannah smiled. If anything could take her mind off her problems, it was one of Miss Fischer's stories about her past.

Chapter Three
Miss Fischer's Jewels

MANY YEARS AGO, when Miss Fischer was a girl, she lived with her father in Berlin. The family was Jewish. All their relations, and many of their friends, were Jewish too. They were happy and hard-working. But when Hitler came to power, he began rounding up the Jews and sending them away to camps in distant parts of the country. Miss Fischer's father saw the terrible danger they were in, and before the soldiers came to get them, he took his daughter and fled. They had to leave behind their house, and all the money they had in the bank. But Mr Fischer had a small collection of very valuable jewels, and these he took with him, hidden in his overcoat.

They came to England, and found a place to live. It was easy for Mr Fischer to find work, with so many young men away at the war. They managed to get by. But they lived in a small, damp, rented flat. For Mr Fischer would not sell his jewels in order to buy a house. A house was no good, he said, if you had to run for your life. You needed something you could carry with you. So he kept his jewels in a box under his bed, until the day he died.

"When I was a child, I never had a horse," Miss Fischer told Hannah. "I never had a garden. Or a house. Or anything. Because my father would not spend his money. Well, your parents didn't hide their money away under the bed, and keep it, as we say in England, for a rainy day. If they had, you would never have had a horse at all. And would that really, do you think, have been better for you, darlink?"

Hannah didn't answer. Miss Fischer carried on.

"When your parents have paid off the loan for the roof, perhaps you will have a horse again."

"By that time," said Hannah, glumly, "I'll be growing up, like Beth, and I won't want a horse, and I'll just flop round the house all day being bored, like you have to when you grow up."

Miss Fischer threw back her head and laughed. Her laugh was huge, like a wave, and it swept you up out of your bad temper.

"Come! Some lemonade!" she said, clapping her hands on her knees, and making them wobble.

But when they went indoors, she forgot about the lemonade. She went past the kitchen and straight into the living room. She opened her piano.

"I play for you!" she cried.

Her hands flew across the keys, and the music burst and bubbled out of the piano. Hannah sat in a big armchair, and all the sadness and anger of the whole day bubbled up like the music. She began to cry. The tears came bursting out of her, and the air came rushing in. She felt as if she was suddenly starting to breathe, like a stone statue coming to life. Her body, which had been so stiff and rigid all day, finally started to relax. Miss Fischer kept on playing.

When at last the music stopped, Miss Fischer said to Hannah, "Better now?"

Hannah nodded.

"Tears are like jewels," Miss Fischer

told her. "It is not good to save them up,
and hide them all away."

Chapter Four
The Gift

AT THREE O'CLOCK the following afternoon, Miss Fischer put on her apron and
rolled up her sleeves. Hannah was coming to tea. At least, that's what she
thought. She didn't realize that she had
forgotten to invite her.

Afternoon tea, it seemed to Miss Fischer, was a very English affair, and that was why she liked it. She never made *kugglehopf* or *strudel*, things she remembered from her childhood days in Germany. It had to be fruit cake, or muffins, or crumpets – something properly English. Today, she was preparing scones. Miss Fischer's scones were famously terrible, as she usually left them in the oven too long, or forgot to add all the ingredients. But she was convinced that they were really rather good.

It was a great pleasure to be making a special tea for such a special young friend. For Hannah was the only person, now, who really liked to hear Miss Fischer's stories of the olden days. She would listen closely, and then go home and think about it, so that the next time they met, she would have lots of interesting questions to ask. Today, she would want to know, for instance, whether Miss Fischer still had her father's jewels.

Miss Fischer rubbed the fat into the flour. No, on second thoughts, Hannah would know, because she was a bright girl, that she hadn't got the jewels any more. Hadn't she said that it was bad to hoard things? She remembered the diamond tiara she had sold to buy her first piano; the gold necklace that had paid for her training as a music teacher; the pocket watch that had gone on her first smart working clothes; and the wonderful brooch that had provided the down-payment for her house here in Cheriston. She remembered her jewels with gratitude and affection, the same way she remembered her father. But she didn't regret that they were gone.

She poured a little milk into the mixing-bowl, and stirred it in. She tipped the dough out on to the table, and a wisp of flour puffed up. She rolled out the dough, and cut it into rounds, which she laid on the baking tray. She put it in the oven, and switched on the gas. Then she remembered something. The jewels were not all gone! There was one brooch left. She had kept it, just in case. Where on earth had she put it? She picked up the matchbox, and took out a match to light the gas. All of a sudden, it came to her –

the brooch was taped to the back of the painting above the sitting room mantelpiece. Yes! She dropped the matches, and bustled through into the sitting room, to see if her brooch was still there. It was.

Miss Fischer held the brooch in the palm of her hand. It had three large diamonds in the middle, with smaller stones, mostly rubies, clustered around them. It was amazing how much a little trinket like that could be worth. Enough to buy a horse. Enough for a new roof. Enough for both of those, and some left over. Miss Fischer didn't need it any more. She was old, and there wouldn't be any more rainy days now.

She found a box in the bureau, and dropped the brooch inside. Then she

wrapped it in blue paper, and attached a
label.

To Hannah – you will know how to use it.
Your friend, Miss Fischer.

 As she worked, she was aware of a faint
smell of gas, coming from the kitchen. In
a minute, she must go and check the
cooker. She hid the present down the
back of her favourite armchair. She wanted it to be a surprise. Then, she felt such
a surge of joy at the thought of making
Hannah happy again, that she simply had
to have music. She sat down, and opened
the piano. Her fingers flew across the
keys, and music filled the room. But it
wasn't only music that filled the room.
Noiselessly, the gas came drifting in

through the open door, invisible and deadly.

Miss Fischer closed her eyes. She was drifting on a sea of music. Her head was swimming. She felt dizzy with the pleasure of it. She felt her fingers slowing down. Now, each note hung on the air, waiting for the next one to come. Heaven could not be more beautiful, Miss Fischer thought. And with that, she passed blissfully on to the next thing, in her usual way, leaving her latest plan sadly uncompleted.

Chapter Five
Brave Hannah

AT ABOUT THE time that Miss Fischer was making her scones, Hannah was walking home from school with her sister. She was still cross with Beth for forgetting about The Terrible Day, especially as Beth wasn't sorry at all.

"He was only a horse!" she kept saying.

Hannah couldn't understand why she was being so unkind. She was often thoughtless – but not usually cruel. Hannah just ignored her, and plodded on. She was still sad, whenever she thought about Sherbert. She was glad to have something else to think about – Miss Fischer and her father's jewels. There were a lot of questions she wanted to ask. How many jewels were there? How big were they? What kind of box did he keep them in? She needed all the details, so that she could picture it in her mind's eye, and imagine it all, the way it really was.

As soon as they got home from school, Hannah took Slobber for a walk. He was really her dad's dog. He had bought him to keep him company on his rounds. But Slobber hated going in the van, and Dad had to leave him at home, so it was Hannah who actually looked after him. She felt guilty about ignoring him the previous day. After all, he was as dear to her as Sherbert, and she had had him an awful lot longer. She might have lost one of her special friends, but she still had the other two, didn't she? She still had Slobber and Miss Fischer. She must be grateful for that.

Slobber went eagerly ahead. They could hear Miss Fischer's piano, as they walked down the road. She seemed to be playing something very slow. Hannah had never heard it before. She stopped for a few seconds to listen, but then Slobber disappeared into someone's garden, and she had to run after him and get him out again.

By the time they got home, Miss Fischer had stopped playing the piano. The garden was quiet. Hannah stood for a while by the old potting-shed. There was a light breeze, and she could hear the brown leaves dropping softly to the ground. She climbed over the wall. Miss Fischer's house was closed and silent. She went up to the back door, and knocked. No answer. She peered into the kitchen. There was flour all over the table. Miss Fischer had been cooking something. Scones, perhaps. Was she expecting someone for tea? Hannah knocked again.

For some reason, she began to feel uneasy. She crossed to the French windows. Now she could see Miss Fischer slumped across the piano. Had she fainted? Had she had a heart attack? With a horrible feeling of dread, Hannah went back to the kitchen door, and turned the handle. She opened the door, and the gas came rushing out. It was overpowering. Hannah took a step backwards, and clapped her hands over her mouth. She felt dizzy, and she thought she might be sick.

Miss Fischer was in the most terrible danger. Hannah took a deep gulp of good fresh air, and then she ran through the gas-filled kitchen, and into Miss Fischer's sitting room, holding her breath all the time. She flung open the French windows, and ran out into the garden again, gasping for air. There was no time to lose. She took another deep breath. Maybe she could pull Miss Fischer out of the house. She ran back inside, with her hand over her mouth. But then she took a proper look at Miss Fischer, lying there across the keys of the piano, and somehow she knew that there was no hurry after all.

"What a splendid girl she is!" thought Miss Fischer's spirit, as she watched Hannah's brave attempts to save her.

She looked down at her own body, and it looked to her like a bag of laundry, propped up on the old piano stool. It was not important, that body. It was no more important than the tin, when you've taken the baked beans out of it. It was something you just threw away. For she felt . . . wonderful! She felt — as indeed, she was — as light as air. She was floating, wafting, flying away towards something new. She was happy that she had given her last precious jewel to Hannah. The child most certainly deserved it.

"Oh, no!" Miss Fischer thought, pulling herself up sharp. "I've done it again!"

She remembered the little box pushed down the back of her favourite chair. No one would ever know it was there. It might be burnt! It might be destroyed! It might be taken off to the rubbish tip! Before she could go anywhere else, she realized, she must make sure that Hannah got her gift.

She couldn't foresee any problems. There was a strong history of haunting in her family. Hardly a night went by in their house in Germany without some dead relative wafting through. Her own dear father had called in for tea at Cheriston once or twice since he passed over. It was a pity she couldn't offer him one of her famous scones any more, but he seemed to cope with his disappointment about that surprisingly well.

She would visit Hannah as soon as possible, and tell her about the brooch. She must do it slowly and gently, in case Hannah was frightened of ghosts. perhaps after supper. It was simply too spooky to go calling on friends in the middle of the night, like ghosts are supposed to do.

Chapter Six

This Haunting Business

HANNAH SPENT THE rest of the afternoon in the old potting-shed, staring at the wall. Everyone knew they must leave her alone. Even Miss Fischer, who was impatient, as ever, to pass on her message, decided she really couldn't intrude on her there.

Hannah's house was empty, except for the dog. Mrs Stone was talking to a policeman in Miss Fischer's front garden, Mr Stone was still at work, and Beth had gone for a walk with her latest boyfriend, Jason. Slobber was lolling around in the kitchen, feeling sorry for himself, because no one was taking any notice of him. Miss Fischer couldn't bear to float around doing nothing until after supper, so she decided to pay him a visit. She could see herself perfectly well – a bit paler than usual, and lot more transparent! – but she didn't know what she looked like to other people, or whether, in fact, they could see her at all. Perhaps you had to learn how to be a ghost. Perhaps it didn't just happen automatically.

She came to Hannah's bedroom window and peered in. It was some years since she had been in there. When Hannah and Beth were younger, she used to babysit for them. But then, one night, she forgot something rather important – she forgot to stay until their parents got home. So that was the end of her babysitting days.

Miss Fischer touched the window pane and her fingers slid through it, as smoothly as they might slide through water. She pushed her arm right in. She was outside, looking at her own arm inside the room. It was extraordinary. She tried to climb up on to the window sill, but her foot fell through the wall. All of a sudden she found herself inside the house, feeling slightly breathless, as if she had jumped into a pool.

On one side of the room was Hannah's bed. Her shelves and beside table. Her wardrobe. All neat and closed up, like Hannah was herself. On the other side, Beth's bed lay partly hidden under a tangle of bedclothes and dirty washing. Miss Fischer was shocked. "Young girls today!" she tutted to herself, as she passed through the door and into the hallway.

There was an oval mirror on the wall above the telephone. Miss Fischer looked into it. To her surprise, there was nothing there. Perhaps a slight mistiness, but that was all. She could hear Slobber at the back door, whining to be let out. It was time for the test. She went in and placed herself right between him and the door. He blinked. Then, with a delighted bark, which said, "Company, at last!", he launched himself at her. The bark changed to a yelp of dismay, as he found himself plunging straight through Miss Fischer, and hitting the back door with a mighty crash. He lay on the doormat, stunned.

Miss Fischer was sorry to have hurt him, but pleased that her little experiment had worked so well. She was obviously visible. This haunting business was a piece of cake! She could hardly wait to get Hannah on her own and have a little chat.

Chapter Seven
A Bit of a Problem

MISS FISCHER'S CHANCE came later in the evening. Hannah was sitting watching television, with Slobber beside her on the settee. Beth was in the kitchen, doing her homework. Their parents were washing up. Miss Fischer popped her head around the open sitting-room door.

"Hello, darlink!" she said, brightly.

Slobber pricked up his ears. Hannah glanced at him and then went back to her programme. Miss Fischer stepped inside.

Now Slobber lifted his head and looked at Miss Fischer. He gave a little whine of pleasure and his tail thumped on the cushions.

"What is it, boy?" Hannah asked, following his gaze. She couldn't see what he was getting so excited about.

"Can't you see me, darlink?" cried Miss Fischer, in dismay.

Slobber stood up on the settee and barked to show Miss Fischer that he cer-

tainly could see her, and very pleased he
was about it, too! He jumped down from
the settee and flung himself joyously at
her. But instead of the soft, silky folds of
Miss Fischer's dress, it was the cold, hard
panels of the wooden door that Slobber
found himself crashing into. Again! It
slammed shut, and Slobber lay, stunned,
on the floor in front of it.

Miss Fischer winced, and said sorry to
the dog, before stepping lightly over him
to go and sit down beside Hannah. She
put her hand on Hannah's arm. It slipped
straight through, and came out the other
side.

"Oh, bother!" cried Miss Fischer.

But Hannah couldn't see or hear her
at all. She jumped up and ran over

to Slobber, going straight through Miss Fischer, and making her feel quite peculiar.

"Are you all right, Slobber?" asked Hannah, putting her arms around his neck.

Then she heard her dad outside the door, asking if anything was wrong. He was rattling the handle, but he couldn't get in. Hannah pulled the dog out of the way.

"What's going on?" her father cried.

"It's Slobber," Hannah said, in a puzzled voice. "He just threw himself against the door."

"What did he do that for?" said her mother, coming in with a tea-towel in her hands.

Hannah shrugged.

"Is there something wrong with him, do you think?" she said, anxiously.

Beth said, "The dog's going senile, that's all."

"What's senile?" Hannah asked.

"Old and silly," said Beth, in an offhand way. "Like your other friends."

"Beth!" said her mother, sharply. "How can you be so horrible to Hannah, when she's having such a terrible time?"

Hannah just stared at them both, blankly. Things were getting too much for her. First Sherbert, then Miss Fischer, and now even Slobber . . .

"She doesn't care!" Beth said. "Look at her. Cool as a cucumber! It's me who's suffering, isn't it?"

"What on earth do you mean?" her father demanded.

"No crisps, no sweets, no pocket-money, no babysitting money, no trips, no discos . . . all because of your rotten old roof." She burst into tears.

"*Our* rotten old roof," her mother corrected her. "We all live in this house." She put her arm across Beth's trembling shoulders. "The thing is, Beth . . . you can't make yourself feel better by making someone else feel worse. Can you?"

"Yes, you can!" Beth shouted, shaking herself free. "You jolly well can!"

And she stormed out of the room, in floods of tears.

Miss Fischer stood in the middle of all this, and not one of them knew she was there. Only Slobber, who kept looking up at her, warily.

"His eyes are rolling up!" cried Hannah. "He's going to die!"

"Don't be silly, dear," her mother said. "He's just upset. Like all of us are. Why don't we put on his favourite video? Come on."

They sat down on the settee, Hannah, her mother and the dog. Hannah's father sat in one of the armchairs. Miss Fischer sat in the other.

"Oh, dear," she thought.

Perhaps this haunting business was actually going to be a bit of a problem after all.

Chapter Eight

Hannah Gets a Cold, and Miss Fischer Has an Idea.

IN THE MIDDLE of the night, Miss Fischer stood by Hannah's bed. If ghosts walk at night, like they're supposed to do, she thought, then perhaps that's because they show up more in the dark. After all, ghosts are generally believed to be white, and she was certainly looking paler than usual. Perhaps she would glow in the dark!

She gave a little cough. Hannah didn't stir. She said Hannah's name. Still, Hannah didn't stir. She took a deep breath and shouted at the top of her voice. But her huge, loud scream came out tiny and small, like the faraway moan of the wind. She stamped on the floor; she jumped up and down. If things go bump in the night, she thought, then how on earth do they do it? It was very vexing. She sat down on the bed. Hannah shivered, and pulled her quilt more tightly around her.

Now, here was an interesting thing.

Could it be that she made the air around her cold? Miss Fischer got up, and crossed to Beth's bed. She leaned over her. Beth nestled down more deeply in her untidy heap of bedclothes, like a little hedgehog in its winter pile of leaves. So, if they couldn't see her, and couldn't hear her, at least they could feel that she was there. She would stay close to Hannah in the morning. Hannah was bound to wonder what was making her chilly. She might think something odd was going on. She might be on the look-out, then, for any little signs Miss Fischer might be able to think up.

It didn't quite work out that way. Hannah shivered so much at the breakfast table, that her mother decided she must have caught a chill. She was sent off to bed with a hot-water bottle and a warm, milky drink. If Hannah thought anything odd was lurking around, she assumed it was an unfriendly germ, and never dreamt that it might be a friendly ghost.

Mrs Stone went to work as usual, but promised to come home as early as she could. She gave Hannah her work number and told her to ring if she had any problems.

"Slobber will look after you," she said. "Are you warm enough?"

Hannah nodded. She was much warmer. But then, Miss Fischer had retreated to the far side of the room and was leaning against the window sill, watching. She would have Hannah and

Slobber to herself for the whole morning. Surely there must be something she could do to make Hannah notice her.

She reached across and touched one of the blusher pots on Beth's bedside table. She tried to push it. Her fingers went straight through. Something smaller then. She tried a scrap of cotton wool. It was no good. There was a heap of talcum powder on the carpet. She crouched down on all fours, and gave a big blow. She pushed with her fingers. Even the tiny grains of powder were solid and immovable to her touch. It was quite depressing. What now? Miss Fischer sat down on Beth's bed, and rested her chin on her hand.

Hannah lay in bed, staring at the ceiling. Slobber kept an eye on Miss Fischer, but he didn't try to jump up any more. He had learnt his lesson about that! Then suddenly Hannah turned her head, and looked straight at Miss Fischer. But she didn't see her. She saw Beth's bed.

Hannah got up and put on her dressing-gown. She went up to Beth's bed. Miss Fischer moved away. Hannah began to push all the dirty clothes and scraps of tissue, and last week's homework, and spilt talcum powder, underneath her sister's bed.

"It's not that I'm cross with her . . ." she told Slobber, as she worked.

Although, of course, she was.

"It's not that I don't like her any more . . ." she said.

Although, of course, she didn't.

She opened the drawer of Beth's bedside cabinet, and swept all the bits of used cotton wool, and the open tubes of face make-up, and the broken eye-pencils into it.

"It's just that I need some space. I need everything to be smooth and clear."

The dog watched her, attentively. He seemed to understand.

"I want to tidy away all the clutter, Slobber. I need to clear away all the bad stuff. I want to have nothing left of it. See?"

She looked around the room. All the surfaces were empty. She pulled the covers straight on Beth's bed. She was satisfied. Now the room was all her own.

"I feel better now," she said to Slobber, fondling his floppy ears. "Stronger."

She thought he understood.

Miss Fischer understood. It occurred to her that she, too, might feel stronger in her own environment. Perhaps that was why ghosts usually appeared in the houses they had lived in, and not on motorways, or in swimming pools, or in other people's homes. If she could somehow get Hannah to come to her house . . .

Hannah lay down on her bed again. She was very tired. Slobber jumped up beside her. He was a big dog, and there was only just room for him.

"Thank goodness I've still got you," she told him. "I just don't know how I could get through all this without you."

She closed her eyes, and very soon she began to doze.

In Miss Fischer's mind, an idea was forming. It was, perhaps, a desperate measure. But pretty soon they would be selling off her furniture. When time was of the essence, then surely desperate measures were called for.

Chapter Nine
So Far So Good

HANNAH WAS SOUND asleep. Slobber lay beside her, with his chin resting on her tummy, looking at Miss Fischer with a quizzical eye. They were old friends, him and Miss Fischer. For it wasn't only Hannah who liked to call on the old lady when times were hard. If he was bored, or lonely, or in disgrace, he would wriggle through the gap at the far end of the garden wall, and she would give him bone-shaped biscuits from his special jar and stroke his head. Now here she was, all of a sudden, in his house. Perhaps times were hard for her. He wanted to make her feel welcome. But, on the other hand, he didn't want to keep smacking into things.

"Hello, darlink," Miss Fischer said to him, softly. He pricked up his ears.

"Would you like a bone biscuit?" she went on.

He sat up on the bed. Hannah rolled over and sighed, in her sleep.

"You come with Miss Fischer," Miss

Fischer said.

Slobber jumped down off the bed.

Miss Fischer was about to take the direct route through the closed window, but she stopped herself just in time, before Slobber had a chance to come crashing through after her. The bedroom door was ajar. She stood back to let him go first. He could pull it open; she couldn't. The kitchen window was open. It was an escape route Slobber often used. They went to the bottom of the garden, and through the gap. Miss Fischer was pleased with herself for remembering he couldn't just slip through things like she could. But then she forgot, and filtered straight through her own back door. Slobber tried to follow her. Bang!

He stood, dazed, on the doormat, shaking his head.

"Sorry darlink," Miss Fischer called, from behind the door. "You wait. I shall open the door."

It was easier said than done. She did feel stronger in her own house. She could move a cobweb with her finger, and in the kitchen mirror, she could clearly see herself – faint and transparent maybe, but more than the wisp of mist she had seen when she looked in the mirror in Hannah's house. If Hannah could be persuaded to come here, Miss Fischer felt certain she would be able to see her. And surely she would search everywhere for Slobber. She needed him. Hadn't she said so? She knew he liked to hang around in

Miss Fischer's house. She was bound to come.

Miss Fischer picked up the back door key; at least she could manage something light like that here. She put it in the lock. But she couldn't get it to turn. Her fingers just kept slipping through it. She could hear Slobber outside, whining to get in. He wasn't the most patient of dogs. She didn't want him to give up on her and go wandering off home.

Well! If she couldn't let him in to get a biscuit, she must take the biscuits out to him. She tried to pick up the jar, but it was too heavy. She managed to pull it slowly across the worktop. It teetered on the edge, and she put her hands underneath to catch it. It toppled over into her hands, dropped straight through them, and smashed into a hundred pieces on the kitchen floor.

Outside the door, Slobber went berserk. He could hear his biscuits, he could smell his biscuits . . . and he wanted to eat his biscuits!

"One moment, darlink!" cried Miss Fischer, snatching up a handful of broken biscuits and making for the door. She slid through it like a knife through butter, but the biscuits, being real and solid, did not. They thudded against the wood, and dropped down on to the doormat, and however hard poor Slobber pressed his nose into the gap under the door, he couldn't even get a nibble of them.

He began to dribble. He was a champion dribbler! They hadn't called him 'Slobber' for nothing!

"Never mind," said Miss Fischer, sitting down on the step beside him. "Soon, Hannah will come, and she will be able to see me here, and I will tell her, 'Get poor Slobber a biscuit!' How does that sound?"

It sounded unconvincing. By the time Hannah came, Miss Fischer would have forgotten all about his biscuits!

Slobber sighed, and looked gloomily up at her.

Miss Fischer gave him a little smile. She was relieved to see that he didn't seem to be going anywhere. So far, so good, she thought.

Chapter Ten
Time Is Running Out

SOME TIME LATER Hannah woke up and found Slobber gone. She didn't get up and go looking for him. It was the last straw. It was more than she could bear. She wanted to cry. At first, she tried to stop herself, by staring hard at the blank walls, and the empty surfaces of the room. But then she remembered what Miss Fischer had said about tears. And she lay in her bed, and let the tears come streaming down her face.

The first one home was Beth. She glanced into the bedroom and saw her bed all smoothed out, and her precious things all gone, and she was furious. She stormed in to have it out with Hannah, but stopped dead when she saw her. She had never in her life seen her sister cry. It shocked her. She had always been such a tough little thing. Beth sat down on the bed, and put her hand on Hannah's arm. She felt guilty about all the horrible things she had said. She felt sorry.

"Where's the Slob?" she asked, gently.

"He's gone!" Hannah sobbed.

"He'll be back," Beth said.

But Hannah just went on crying.

Meanwhile, Miss Fischer was sitting patiently in her garden with Slobber, waiting for Hannah to come. She tried to make Slobber bark. But he didn't feel like barking, and you could never make him do anything he didn't want to do. Eventually, Miss Fischer went and looked in Hannah's window to see if she was awake yet. She saw the two girls on Hannah's bed, crying on each other's shoulders. She was horrified. What had she done? She called to Slobber. She would have to find some other way of making Hannah come to her house.

Miss Fischer led Slobber right back

into Hannah's room. On her way out again, she noticed the local paper, lying on the doormat. The back page was all notices of auction sales. There was a picture of Miss Fischer's house. *Sale of House and Contents*, it said underneath. *Date, Tuesday, 9th October. Viewing, Monday 2-5pm.*

She had only one week left, before some stranger would come and buy her old armchair, and take away with him Hannah's wonderful gift! Time was running out!

Chapter Eleven
The Viewing

THE WEEK FLEW past. Miss Fischer tried everything she could think of to make Hannah notice her. She jumped up and down on the television, making the picture go wobbly. She blew as hard as she could on the radio, making the sound go fuzzy. She turned hot drinks cold, by putting her hands around the cup, and she took the warmth out of the fire by standing in front of it. But it was no good. The sole result of all her efforts was that Mr Stone decided the house was awfully draughty, and stuck strips of sellotape round all the doors and windows.

Monday morning came, and Miss Fischer thought her only chance was to play for time. If she could frighten the people who came to the viewing, then they wouldn't want to come back and buy anything. So when the agent put his sign up outside her door – *Sale here tomorrow. Viewing now on* – and opened up the house, Miss Fischer was ready and waiting.

People kept coming all through the afternoon. Men in suits, and men in dungarees. Women in hats, and in jeans. Little children, who fingered the lace chair-covers and the tasselled curtains. Babies who dribbled on the carpets.

Miss Fischer flitted between the rooms, in what she hoped was a ghostly way. But the only ones who seemed to notice her comings and goings were the children. The babies chuckled. The toddlers pointed and giggled. An older boy, who was off school with a tummy ache, actually struck up a conversation with her. His mother, seeing him apparently chatting to a dining-room chair, thought he must be getting a fever, and wanted to take him home. But his father just said,

"Leave him alone. It's just a pretend game, isn't it? You know what kids are like!" And he went back to examining Miss Fischer's crystal chandelier. Miss Fischer jumped up on to a chair and pushed the crystals with her hand. They swayed slightly. There was a faint jingling sound. The man took a step back, and eyed it suspiciously. The boy laughed.

If the grown-ups couldn't see her, Miss Fischer thought, she would just have to start to mingle with them a bit. She made them shiver as she passed among them. She touched the piano keys and people turned their heads and frowned. She fluttered the pages of sheet music. She rustled the leaves of her prize aspidistra.

Everybody who came to her house

that day left it uneasy, or even alarmed. There was something spooky about it. They didn't want anything from that eerie house. Who would buy a piano that tinkled like that, all on its own? Who would buy a pot-plant that stirred and rustled, even when there wasn't any breeze? And who would want to stand through hours of bidding, in a house that made their flesh creep?

But there was one person at the viewing who was completely unaware of these ghostly goings-on. It was Mrs Stone. And she was unaware of Miss Fischer's antics for the simple reason that Miss Fischer kept well away from her. If Mrs Stone was planning to come to the sale the next day, there was always a

chance that she might decide to bid for
the old armchair. It was a very small
chance. But, by now, Miss Fischer was
clutching at straws.

Mrs Stone wasn't looking for furniture. Her house was full to bursting
already. What she was looking for was
some small memento of Miss Fischer –
something for Hannah to remember her
by. There were ornaments and bowls on
the mantelpiece. Perhaps one of those
would do. A pair of porcelain dogs in the
fireplace. An old-fashioned table lamp.
She wandered across to the piano. There
were lots of things on it, crammed
together, ready for the sale.

Among them, she found the very
thing. It was a small wooden box, with a

metal clasp. Hannah would like that. She had boxes of every shape and size stacked away in her cupboard. She kept all her bits and pieces in them. She needed them, because she hated to leave things lying around.

"Seen anything you fancy?" the agent asked Mrs Stone, as she was leaving.

"Just one thing," she replied. "A little box . . ."

Miss Fischer groaned. There was noting more she could do. It was out of her hands now. But it was not in her nature to be gloomy for very long. She would stay around for the sale, and if some stranger bought the chair, she would move on. On to the next thing. That had always been her way.

Chapter Twelve
Miss Fischer's Moment of Triumph

THE NEXT DAY, being Tuesday, Hannah should have gone to school. But when her mother told her about the little wooden box, she got very excited, and said she simply had to see it. It could be

The Box – the one Miss Fischer's father had hidden his jewels in, when he had brought his family out of Germany. She remembered the last time she had seen Miss Fischer, and all the questions she had wanted to ask. Now she would never know what had happened to the jewels, or whether Miss Fischer had any of them left. But if she could see the box and hold it, perhaps she would somehow get a sense of what had happened.

So Hannah and her mother went early to the sale, arriving there before anyone else, and having time for a good look around. Hannah felt strange, being back in the house now that Miss Fischer was gone. She stood silently in the sitting room as the people began to arrive. There weren't many people. The auctioneer said he couldn't understand why it was such a poor turn-out.

Miss Fischer's table linen and her best tea set were the first things to go. They weren't particularly familiar to Hannah. She watched with interest as the sale went on, and things she had never seen before came under the hammer. And then the auctioneer got to the ornaments on the piano. Hannah looked at the piano and the empty piano stool. She remembered all the times Miss Fischer had played for her, and she missed her. The feeling was so strong and sudden, it made her catch her breath. It was like a real pain. She longed to see Miss Fischer . . .

And then – she could see her! Sitting

on the piano stool, looking exactly the same as ever. Well, except that she was transparent, of course.

"Miss Fischer!" Hannah gasped.

"What, dear?" said Mrs Stone.

"Miss Fischer – loved that piano," Hannah said, staring at the old lady.

"Darlink!" said Miss Fischer, delightedly. "I've been trying to get through to you for days!"

The auctioneer tapped his hammer, and moved on to the next item. It was the little box.

"Do you think that box might have belonged to Miss Fischer's father?" Hannah whispered to her mother, hoping that Miss Fischer would give her the answer.

"Maybe . . ." her mother said.

"No," said Miss Fischer. "Now, listen, darlink. I have something important to tell you . . ."

Hannah said, softly, "What was that one like – the one he kept the jewels in?"

The auctioneer said, "Two pounds here . . . two pounds fifty, the lady in the corner . . . you, madam, three pounds . . ."

Hannah's mother was too busy bidding for the box to notice Hannah any more.

"I said, I have something important to tell you," Miss Fischer repeated. "So don't change the subject or I might forget what it was!"

Hannah grinned. Miss Fischer said, "You must buy the chair. You know – my favourite armchair. I wish you to have it."

This didn't seem to Hannah to be such a very important message. What on earth did she want a moth-eaten old chair for? Weren't there much more exciting things to talk about, under the circumstances?

"What's it like being dead?" Hannah asked.

"I don't know, dear," said her mother, who had managed to outbid everyone else, and was now the proud owner of Miss Fischer's little box.

". . . and now we come," said the auctioneer, "to this fine old armchair. Who will start the bidding? Who will give me three pounds?'

Hannah put up her hand.

"Good girl!" cried Miss Fischer, who

had jumped up on to the table in excitement.

"Hannah!" said Mrs Stone. "What on earth are you doing?"

"I want the chair," said Hannah.

"But we haven't got room for it," her mother objected.

"Three pounds fifty, you sir . . ." said the auctioneer. "And am I bid four pounds?"

Hannah raised her hand again.

"I've got that lovely little box for you, Hannah," Mrs Stone reminded her. "Surely you don't need an ugly great chair as well?"

"Four pounds fifty, the man in blue . . . five pounds, anyone?"

Hannah raised her hand.

"Yes, yes!" cried Miss Fischer, tap dancing on air.

She was still as fat, and still as lively, but lighter now, and her tiny feet no longer looked too small to hold her up.

"Five pounds. Five pounds for the chair . . ." The auctioneer scanned the crowd. "Five pounds fifty, anyone? No? Then it's five pounds once, five pounds twice . . . five pounds, to the little girl in green!"

"Yes! Yes! Yes!" yelled Miss Fischer, joy-fully.

She had done it! The chair was safe! She knew that Hannah would never part with it. It, and everything in it, was hers. Hers, forever.

"Got to fly, darlink!" cried Miss

Fischer, impatient as ever to be moving on.

And, with that, she shot up into the air and disappeared through the ceiling, leaving Hannah staring after her, open-mouthed.

"Oh, bother!" Miss Fischer thought, as she went sailing up. "I remembered to tell her to buy the chair, but I forgot to tell her why!"

But it was too late now. She simply couldn't bear to hang around any longer!

Chapter Thirteen
Beth Makes a Discovery

HANNAH PUT THE chair in her bedroom, and sat down on it. She wondered why Miss Fischer had wanted her to have it so much. It seemed an odd choice. Why not the jar she had kept Slobber's bone biscuits in? Why not the mugs they had drunk hot chocolate from so many times?

"Why did you want me to have this chair in particular?" she asked softly.

But nobody answered. Miss Fischer had gone.

Hannah sat in her chair, and it was curiously comforting. She was glad she had bought it. She loved it already. Not that she expected Beth to love it, too. It really did clutter up the bedroom.

"I'm sorry, Beth," she said, when her sister came home from school. "I know it takes up a lot of room. But I wanted it so much . . ."

"No problem!" said Beth, flopping down on her bed. "There's going to be pots of room around here from now on, because I've decided to keep my things tidy!"

Hannah was speechless with surprise.

"No, really," Beth went on. "I've been a pig! But it never occurred to me you minded about my mess. You never said anything about it, did you? But then, you never say anything about anything. You don't have tempers and tantrums like the rest of us do, so sometimes it seems as if nothing matters to you."

Hannah stared at her in astonishment.

"That's why I got fed up with you, actually," added Beth. "I mean, I was suffering, and I didn't really see why you shouldn't suffer too."

"What do you mean?" asked Hannah.

"Well . . . when we got our pocket

money stopped because of the rotten old roof, and I threw a wobbler, you just . . . you just accepted it. And that made me feel even worse."

"It doesn't mean I wasn't angry too."

"I know that now. But then you didn't even get stressed about Sherbert, and I thought you just didn't have any feelings at all. I mean, if I'd loved that horse as much as you did, I'd have hit the roof about them wanting to sell him! I wouldn't just have let them! So you going quietly off to the potting-shed just made me feel like . . . well . . . like some sort of frantic freak."

"Sorry," Hannah said. "I had no idea."

"Me neither," said Beth, giving her a smile.

"What're we going to do then?" asked Hannah. "It's no good expecting me to have tantrums and stuff – I just can't!"

"I know. But you could say how you feel, couldn't you?"

Hannah nodded.

"And I could try to listen!" said Beth. "That's not easy for me, you know!" She stood up. "But first I'm going to do something else that's not easy for me . . ."

Hannah watched her sister take off her school uniform, and hang it in the wardrobe. Yes! She hung it in the wardrobe! She watched her take some clothes from the heap on the floor, picking off the bits of used tissue, and the little balls of hair she had cleaned from her brush some days before. Then came the big spring clean.

Beth put the lids on all her bottles and tubes, and lined them up neatly on the shelf above her bed. She folded some of the clothes on the floor and put them in her drawer. She took her prized collection of dirty underwear and put it in the washing machine. She ventured into the dark regions under the bed, where old toffees lurked, all covered in dust. She retrieved a fossilized dough-nut. She even brought in her age-old enemy, the vacuum cleaner.

By tea-time the bedroom was trans-formed. Hannah, who thought this was what she had always wanted, was oddly disappointed. She was touched that Beth had wanted to please her but now the room was too clean, too clear, and Hannah missed the chaos and disorder that was so much part of Beth. After a few days, she was starting to plant things on Beth's side of the room – a dirty sock here – an open tube of make-up there – as if the whole heap might grow again from that. But Beth always tidied these little seeds of messiness away.

Before Christmas, the builders came and mended the roof. The weather was dry and cold. To Hannah's relief, Beth was beginning to slip back into her old ways. A discreet scattering of knickers and tissues could be seen on the bedroom floor, like a light covering of snow. The make-up came down from the shelf. Beth had another new boyfriend, and she couldn't concentrate on anything else. It was love! Her side of the bedroom erupted once again.

So it was that, on the night of the Year Ten Christmas disco, Beth was frantically searching among her things for her Iced Blackberry lipstick. She burrowed and rummaged, scattering debris behind her, like Slobber scattering earth from the flowerbeds on one of his bone hunts.

"Have you had it, Hannah?" she demanded, desperately.

"Of course not," Hannah said.

"Can I look in your things?"

"Be my guest."

Beth searched Hannah's drawers and shelves. She slid her hand down the back of Hannah's chair.

"There's something here!" she cried.

She brought out Miss Fischer's little surprise. She read the label.

"It's a present from Miss Fischer! She must've forgotten to give it to you!"

Hannah tore the blue paper off it, with trembling fingers. Beth called their mother.

"What's up?" she said, appearing in the doorway.

Hannah stood by the window, holding the brooch in the palm of her hand. The three big diamonds sparkled in the yellow December sun. They were so bright, they made her eyes water.

"It's nice . . ." Beth said. "A bit old-fashioned, of course . . ."

"It's a token of Miss Fischer's affection," said their mother. "That's what counts."

"It's more than that," Hannah told them both. "I think it may be worth a lot of money."

She told them the story of Miss Fischer's flight from Germany, with her father and his jewels. They listened patiently.

"Hannah, dear," her mother said at last, "I'm afraid that's all just an old lady's romantic notions . . . She was a bit confused, you know, towards the end. They can't be real diamonds. Nobody has diamonds as big as that."

"But it was a lovely story," Beth added.

Then she started her search again. She

97

never found the Iced Blackberry. She had
to settle for the Crushed Strawberry, in
the end.

Chapter Fourteeen
The Three Diamonds

EARLY THE NEXT morning, Hannah pinned the brooch to her jacket and set off to catch the bus. Her plan was to look in all the jewellers' shops in Cheriston High Street, and see what a brooch like hers would cost to buy. She didn't believe

for one moment that Miss Fischer was
confused. And she didn't think she was a
fraud, either. In which case, the brooch
simply couldn't be a fake, could it?

But there was nothing similar in any of
the jewellers' shops' windows. She would
have to go into one and ask. The man in
Perryman's looked the most approach-
able, so that was where she went.

"Do you . . . value things?" she asked
him.

"Yes," he said. "But we have to make a
charge, of course."

Hannah was crestfallen.

"I haven't got any money," she told
him.

She had spent her savings on Miss
Fischer's chair, and she hadn't had any

pocket-money since the roof began to leak.

"What is it that you want valued?" the man said, kindly, taking pity on her. "Perhaps I could just have a little look at it."

She took off the brooch. The man put on his spectacles, and clipped a magnifying glass over one of the lenses. He examined the brooch for a few seconds, and then he let out a long, low whistle.

★

When Hannah told her parents how much the brooch was worth, they were astounded.

"What are you going to do with it?" her mother asked.

"Sell it," said her father, immediately,

"and put the money in the bank, I should say."

But Hannah shook her head. She thought she knew what Miss Fischer would have wanted her to do with it. The same thing she must have done herself, all those years before, when she became the owner of her father's jewels.

"I'm going to break it up," she said. "One of these diamonds will buy me a horse, and his stabling fees for life. That's something I really want. One of them will pay off the bank loan for the roof, so we'll be able to have treats and pocket-money again. That's something we really need."

"Hear, hear!" Beth agreed heartily.

"What about the last one?" said her mum.

"The last one I'm going to put in that little box you got me at Miss Fischer's auction sale, and keep it under the bed."

"Under the bed?" exclaimed her father. "What's wrong with the bank?"

"In an emergency," Hannah told him, "you can't always get to the bank, can you? You need something small, that you can carry with you."

"But, Hannah . . ."

Hannah wasn't listening any more. She looked at the three diamonds. Soon, there would be only one left. But the other two would not be lost. They would simply be exchanged, one for a horse, and the other for the new roof. Not so long ago, she had had three special friends. Now there was only one left. But the other two were not lost. Nothing was ever lost. Their love, and all the things they taught her, would be part of her life forever.